JOE USELESS

For Joe and Alice

First published in Great Britain in Picture Lions 1993
Picture Lions is an imprint of the Children's Division,
part of HarperCollins Publishers Limited,
77-85 Fulham Palace Road,
Hammersmith, London W6 8JB

Text and illustrations copyright © Dennis Reader 1993

A CIP catalogue record for this book is available
from the British Library.
The author asserts the moral right to be identified as
the author of the work.

ISBN: 0 00 664258-6

Printed in Great Britain

This book is set in 18/22 New Baskerville

JOE USELESS

• Dennis Reader •

PictureLions

An Imprint of HarperCollins*Publishers*

Bernard Blossom often wished he had a dog just like his friends.

Jason Potter had a sort of German shepherd...

Desmond Blofeld had a sort of big boxer dog...

Dylan Evans had a sort of shaggy sheepdog – at least that's what people thought it was...

Carmen Biggins had a cat which she said loved her very much...

...and Bernard Blossom had a tortoise.

His friends would throw balls and sticks and run and jump with their dogs.

Even Carmen Biggins would sometimes manage to unhook her cat from her sweater and stroke its glossy coat.

Bernard Blossom's tortoise was a bit boring.

In the summer it ate lettuce leaves. That was quite exciting.

But in the winter when the tortoise slept Bernard only had a cardboard box to look at. That was boring.

One day (and it wasn't
even Bernard's birthday)
his mother and father
surprised him with a
mysterious crackly,
crinkly present.

Bernard undid the wrapping paper. He hoped the present wasn't any more sleepy tortoises.

It was a big basket.

"What's this for?" asked Bernard.

"It's for him!" said his father. In the doorway was a DOG!
A sausage-shaped polony sort of dog.

A funny frankfurter sort of dog.
But it was *his* dog! He would
call him Joe.

The day was sunny and warm. All his friends would be in the park showing off with their dogs. Now it was Bernard's turn.

"Jump, boy, jump!" called Jason Potter and his dog caught a ball with one bound.

"Jump, boy, jump!" called Bernard Blossom and threw the ball. Joe jumped – as high as a blade of grass.

"Here, boy, here!" called Dylan Evans. His dog put his big feet on Dylan's chest and licked his ears.

"Here, boy, here!" called Bernard Blossom. Joe put his front feet on Bernard's toes and wagged his tail.

"Allez!" called Desmond
Blofeld and his dog sprang
through a hoop.

"Allez!" called Bernard
Blossom. Joe tried, but
the hoop got in the way.

"You'll have to get him a set of stilts," laughed Bernard's friends.

"Perhaps his legs will grow one day," called Carmen Biggins.

Bernard sat on his bed. It had been a rotten day. His friends
had laughed at him – and at Joe. He was a useless dog.
 "You'd better come in, useless," said Bernard to Joe.

"You can't catch balls, you can't jump through hoops,
in fact you can't jump at all. You're useless," said Bernard.
"Tomorrow we'll stay away from the park and my friends."

No one ever went to the field behind the old school.
"We'll be on our own," said Bernard.

"We are going to learn to jump!" said Bernard. "Soon
you'll soar through the air." But Joe's legs wouldn't jump
and his belly got in the way.

Then a loud scream and a screech from round the corner
made them both jump.

"Their big dogs chased my beautiful cat into that pipe,"
howled Carmen Biggins. "Now she's stuck in the middle."
The pipe shook and a scratchy noise came from inside.

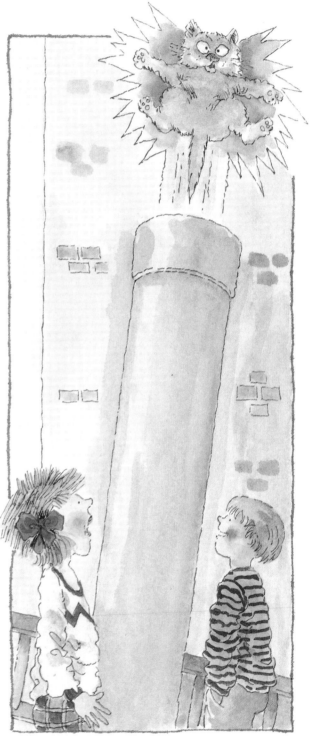

"Where's Joe?" said Bernard.
"Where's my cat?" said Carmen.

"There's your cat," said Bernard.

"Rescued by a sausage-shaped polony sort of dog."
Bernard felt very proud. "He's not so big as the other
dogs – but he's useful."

"I like your dog best, anyway," said Carmen. "He's my hero."

It was bedtime, the end of a perfect day.

"A warm, friendly, cosy sort of dog, that's what you are," said Bernard. "A useful sort of dog..." And then they both went to sleep.